Theo
At the Seaside

This book belongs to

_____

who has a great sense of smell, unlike Theo!

Theo
At the Seaside

Published in the United Kingdom by Smellessence.

© 2013 Smellessence Ltd.

Part of the Bonnier Publishing Group www.bonnierpublishing.com

Appledram Barns, Birdham Road,

Chichester, West Sussex, PO20 7EQ

Written by Jaclyn Crupi

Illustrations by Aurélia Verdoux

Illustrations and text © 2013 Smellessence Ltd

Scents © Celessence

celessence™

Scent technology by Celessence™

10 9 8 7 6 5 4 3 2 1

Follow your nose, just like Theo...

Today the sun is shining. Theo wakes up eager to enjoy the day.

"I would like to go to the **seaside**", he thinks.

"I just love running on the hot sand...

Fetching sticks from the water...

and smelling the salty sea air."

Theo takes a deep sniff, but he smells nothing.

Theo has lost his sense of smell. He cannot smell anything at all!

He **sniffs**, he **inhales**, he **whiffs**.

His sense of smell is missing!

Where can it be?

Theo feels sure that he will find his sense of smell at the seaside.

There are so many delicious smells that can be found there.

He hopes one of them will **wake up** his nose.

Theo trots down the boardwalk. He tries to follow his nose but it's no use - his nose just isn't working.

He follows his stomach instead and it leads him to a candyfloss stand. Theo puts his nose as close to the sticky, sweet treat as he can and breathes in deeply.

He **wiggles** his nose.
Theo takes quick breaths.
Then he takes deep breaths.

Can you smell the sweet candyfloss scent?

9

But Theo smells nothing. No odour, no scent, no fragrance: nothing!

Soon his snout, whiskers and mouth
are covered with sticky candyfloss.

"Where is my sense of smell?" Theo wonders.
"Where could it be?"

Theo *races* over to a beach towel that he
spots on the sand to clean his sticky face.

Just as he's about to wipe his face on the
towel he steps on a bottle of suntan lotion,

and squirts it all over himself.

Oh dear!

Can you smell the suntan lotion's scent?

13

Theo sniffs and whiffs the suntan lotion. He takes **short** breaths. Then takes **long** breaths. But he smells nothing.

No odour, no scent, no aroma; nothing at all. "And now I am covered in candyfloss and sticky lotion" he thinks to himself.

"Where is my sense of smell?"

"Where could it be?"

Theo decides that it is time to head home. He runs down the beach but doesn't get far before he comes across a patch of long grass. Soon Theo is completely tangled in it.

The suntan lotion and candyfloss are so sticky that the grass clings to his fur.

Theo works hard to get unstuck.

Theo remembers how lovely grass smells. He sniffs and whiffs it. He rolls in it. He breathes in and out quickly, but he smells nothing.

No smell,
no scent.
nothing!

Can you smell the grassy scent?

Theo is sticky and dirty and all of this
sniffing has made him tired.

"Time to go home for a bath!" he thinks.

At home, Theo jumps straight
into a bubble bath.

SPLASH!

The bubbles surround him.
He licks them and tries to
catch them on his paw.

Theo may not have found his sense of smell today but he's had a lot of fun at the seaside. He snuggles up in bed with his rubber ducky and falls into a deep sleep.

Until he follows his nose next time...

Join Theo on all his smelly (or not so smelly for him) adventures.

You might have to find him first.